Ira and Jerry's Jelly Ice-cream Sundae

Om KIDZ

An imprint of Om Books International

Om KIDZ | Om Books International

Reprinted in 2023

Corporate & Editorial Office
A-12, Sector 64, Noida 201 301
Uttar Pradesh, India
Phone: +91 120 477 4100
Email: editorial@ombooks.com
Website: www.ombooksinternational.com

Sales Office
107, Ansari Road, Darya Ganj
New Delhi 110 002, India
Phone: +91 11 4000 9000
Email: sales@ombooks.com
Website: www.ombooks.com

ISBN: 978-93-52760-27-5

Printed in India

10 9 8 7 6 5 4 3 2

Ira and Jerry's Jelly Ice-cream Sundae

Paste your photograph here

My name is

It is yet another hot day. **Jerry** and **Ira** are tired of being **indoors**.

They **jump** around **in** the bedroom.

They try **jogging in** the living room.

Both of them are very bored. They stay **inside** and watch TV.

"**I** have an **idea**!
Let us **invent** something,"
says **Ira** all of a sudden.

Jerry thinks about **it**.

“What can we **invent**?” he asks.

"Let's see what we have **in** the fridge," says **Ira**. She goes **into** the kitchen. **Jerry joins** her.

They peek **into** the fridge.
There **is** a **jug** of **juice in it**.
There are also many types of
jams and **jellies in** the fridge.

The freezer **is** full of **ice.**

There **is** milk **in** the freezer.

"Let us make a list of the things we have," says **Jerry**.

He takes a piece of paper.
He writes down all the **items** they have with an **ink** pen.

"What **if** we **invent** a new kind of **ice-cream**?" asks **Ira**. **Jerry** agrees.

In a big bowl, they mix together the milk and **jam**.

Then they add pieces of **jelly** to **it**. They take turns mixing **it**.

Finally, they put the bowl **in** the freezer.

In a few hours, their new **ice-cream is** ready!

They eat **it** with a spoon. They **invite** their mom and dad to try **it** too. They call **it Ira** and **Jerry's jelly ice-cream** sundae.

Know your words

Naming words

ink	ice	jug
Ira	items	juice
idea	ice-cream	jams
Jerry	jellies	

Describing words

indoors inside

Doing words

jumping	joins	invite
jogging	invent	

Sight words

it is into

Circle the things that you would put in an ice-cream.

Find the given words in the word search below.

I	C	E	C	R	E	A	M
G	I	I	Y	K	L	H	I
D	M	N	N	J	N	L	A
J	R	E	L	V	A	Q	B
P	J	U	I	C	E	M	K
O	U	E	H	V	V	N	H
J	E	L	L	I	E	S	T
Y	F	E	A	B	D	B	W

INVENT

JAM

JELLIES

JUICE

ICECREAM

Change one letter of the following words to make new words.

Join - ____________

Jog - ____________

Jam - ____________

Jug - ____________